HOW THE SUN WAS MADE

WHY THE MOON APPEARS AT NIGHT

HOW PEOPLE WERE GIVEN FIRE

RETOLD BY MARGARET MAYO
ILLUSTRATED BY TONY ROSS

ORCHARD BOOKS

ORCHARD BOOKS
96 Leonard Street, London EC2A 4RH
Orchard Books Australia
14 Mars Road, Lane Cove, NSW 2066
ISBN1 86039 699 2 (hardback)
ISBN 1 86039 866 9 (paperback)
First published in Great Britain in **1998**
Text © Margaret Mayo 1995
Illustrations © Tony Ross 1998
The rights of Margaret Mayo to be identified as the author
and Tony Ross as the illustrator of this work
have been asserted by them in accordance with the
Copyright, Designs and Patents Act, 1988.
A CIP catalogue record for this book
is available from the British Library.
Printed in Great Britain

HOW THE SUN
WAS MADE

In the long-ago Dreamtime, when the world was being made, there was no sun in the sky. The only light came from the moon and stars, so everywhere was always dark and gloomy-grey.

At that time, there were no people. They had not yet been made by Biame, the Great Spirit. But there were lots of birds and animals. They were all much bigger than they are today, and much fiercer and more quarrelsome.

Some of the quarrels were caused by the animals and birds bumping into each other in the gloomy-grey darkness. Eagle and Emu's big quarrel, which had such a surprising ending, started like that.

It happened that Eagle was swooping down to catch a little bird for his supper, and, in the gloomy-grey dark, he bumped into Emu, who was strolling along minding his own business. They were both furious. They screamed and screeched, and a fight began.

There was a great flurry of feathers as Eagle pecked and clawed, while Emu tried to kick him. Finally Eagle managed to tug out a whole clump of Emu's tail feathers, and Emu gave one of his powerful back kicks and hit Eagle really hard. This made Eagle so angry that he did the most wicked thing he could think of – he flew off to Emu's nest, snatched up a big egg in his claws and hurled the egg into the air.

Emu's egg flew up and up, *right to the sky*, and landed on a pile of wood that Biame and his spirit helpers had built. With a great *crack!* the egg broke and the golden yolk poured out, *and the wood was set alight!* There were just a few tiny flames at first, but they soon grew into a curling, swirling, leaping mass of red and pink and gold. And that was the first bonfire in the sky – *and it lit up the world below.*

The birds and animals were amazed by this new dazzling light. For the first time, they could see things clearly, and instead of feeling quarrelsome they felt happy and peaceful inside.

Biame and his spirit helpers were amazed too. For the first time, they were able to see how beautiful the world they were making had become. They noticed how happy the birds and animals now were, and that pleased them.

When the fire died down, Biame looked at the gloomy-grey, dark world and he said, "We must make another bonfire in the sky!"

Then Biame asked his spirit helpers to
collect more wood and build another fire
and light it. And this was done – and so it
has continued. Every time a new fire is lit,
it is morning on earth and a new day
begins. When the flames blaze up to their
hottest and brightest, it is midday, and
when the fire dies down and the embers
glow, it is evening.

Now the birds and animals loved the new bright daytime. But there was one problem. Some of them were such deep sleepers that they didn't wake till it was midday or even later, and they were very annoyed at missing so many daylight hours.

Biame thought about this, and he decided to hang a bright star, the morning star, in the eastern sky, just before the fire was lit, to warn everyone that day was coming.

Now the birds were light sleepers, and the star woke them. But most of the animals still went on sleeping. So Biame thought again, and he decided to ask Kookaburra, who had the loudest voice of any bird, to help him.

One of Biame's spirit helpers was sent down to the world in order to find Kookaburra. And it didn't take long. That loud laugh of his – "Gour-gour-gah-gah!" could be heard from a great way off.

"Kookaburra," said the spirit helper, "Biame has work for you. Will you wake every day, when the morning star is first hung in the sky? And then will you laugh your happy laugh and wake everyone?"

"I will!" said Kookaburra. He was very proud to be asked. "Of course I will!"

And Kookaburra kept his promise. Even now he wakes each day, soon after the morning star is hung in the sky. He ruffles his feathers, and waits. The moment the bonfire in the sky is lit, he opens his big beak, and he laughs – "Gour-gour-gah-gah!" And it is such a loud laugh that even the really deep sleepers wake up, ready to enjoy the new day.

(A story told by Australian Aborigines)

WHY THE MOON
APPEARS AT NIGHT

At the beginning, there was darkness and endless water, and in that water lived the ancient god Nun, and his only son, Ra. But there was also an underworld, deep down below, and in that underworld was the fierce and enormous snake, Apep.

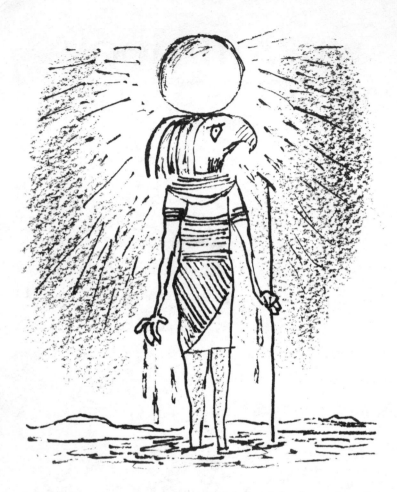

A time came when Ra decided to leave his father. "I shall be the golden sun," said Ra. Then, shining brightly, like the sun, he slowly rose out of the water.

He was a handsome god, very tall, with the body, legs and arms of a man and the feathered head of a hawk. And, at all times and everywhere, he shone brightly.

Now when Ra came out of the water, there was nowhere for him to stand. He thought, and a mound of earth appeared.

He stood on the mound, and he thought some more. First he thought of air, and a soft breeze blew. Ra named him the god Shu. Ra thought of moisture, and a light misty cloud floated by. Ra named her the goddess Tefnut.

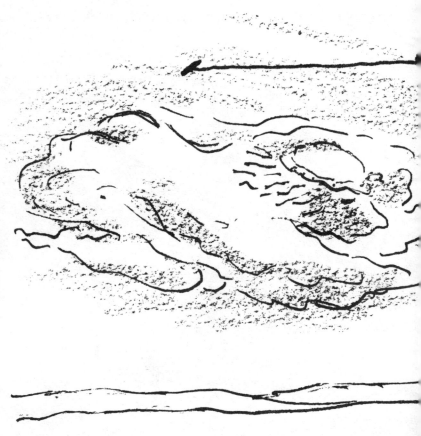

Next Ra made another god and named him Geb. "You shall be the earth," said Ra. And Geb lay down and became the flat earth. He bent his knees and crooked his elbows, and they became mountains and valleys.

21

Then Ra made an exceedingly beautiful goddess and named her Nut. "You shall be the sky," said Ra.

And the beautiful Nut arched her body over the earth. Balancing herself on her toes and fingertips, she stretched and

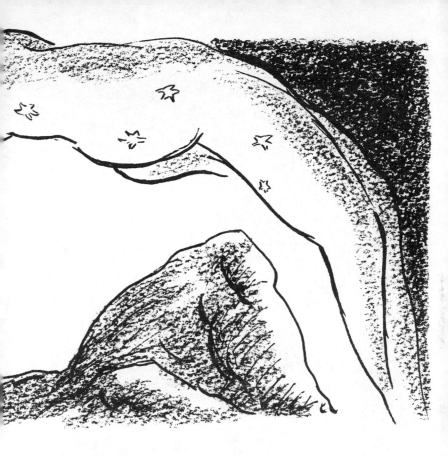

stretched, until the great wide arch of the
sky became.

When Ra saw how beautiful the
goddess Nut was, he made stars and
sprinkled them over her, like jewels, so
that she would be even more beautiful.

Ra thought again, and he wept big
tears, and from each tear sprang a living
being – men and women, all the creatures
that walk, creep, swim or fly, and the
plants that live among them. Ra wept and
wept, until he had made everything that
has life.

Then began a time of peace and happiness. Men, women and children were content, and they worshipped Ra, their shining god, and he ruled over them and was their first Pharaoh. There were never any quarrels or fights. Even the crocodiles hadn't learnt how to snap and bite, nor had the snakes learnt how to sting.

But after a while the animals forgot the ways of peace and began to attack each other. Men, women and children too began to quarrel and hurt each other; they forgot about Ra, their shining god, and stopped worshipping him.

Then Ra was sad. "Why do you have
to quarrel and fight?" he asked. "Why
can't you be friends and live together
peacefully?" But the people took no notice
of Ra, their shining god, and no one
answered.

Ra thought.

"I no longer wish to live in this world," he said. And he rose, up and up, into the sky, where a boat was waiting for him.

He climbed aboard, and off he sailed, across the sky. When he reached the earth's edge, he sailed into the underworld. Then it was dark on earth for the first time. But Ra did not want the people to be afraid. He thought, and he made the moon, so that there would be some soft, silvery light to comfort the people when night came.

Since that time, every day Ra rides in
his boat across the blue sky and shines
upon the earth. In the evening, he sinks
below, into the underworld, and there
waiting for him, is the fierce and
enormous snake, Apep. Every night Apep
coils himself around Ra and his boat and
tries to swallow them.

There is always a long struggle, but Ra is always the stronger. Each morning, without fail, he returns as a golden disc, shining fresh and bright in the eastern sky. And a new day begins.

(An Egyptian story)

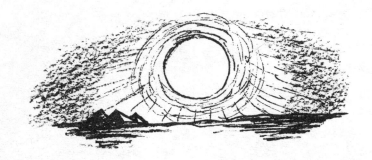

HOW PEOPLE WERE GIVEN FIRE

A long, long time ago, all fire belonged to three Fire Beings who kept it hidden in their tepee, high on a mountain-top. They would not share the fire with anyone, and guarded it carefully, night and day.

So, when winter came and the fierce winds howled and snow covered the earth, men, women and children had no way of warming themselves. No fire. No hot food. Nothing at all.

Now Coyote, who is wise, knew about fire, and one year at winter's end, when he saw how cold and miserable the people were, he decided to steal some fire and give it to them. But how would he do it?

Coyote thought hard.

He called a meeting of the animals, and
he said, "Who will help me steal some fire
and give it to the people?" And Bear,
Deer, Squirrel, Chipmunk and Frog
offered to help.

Coyote thought again.

"Bear," he said, "you are big and strong, so you must come with me to the Fire Beings' tepee. Deer, Squirrel and Chipmunk, you are fast runners, so you must wait beside the trail, ready to run."

"What about me?" asked Frog. "I'd like to help!"

"Fr-og," sighed Coyote, shaking his head, "you're such a squatty little thing. You can jump and swim, but you can't run. There's nothing you can do."

"I could wait by the pond and be ready," said Frog. "Just in case..."

"You do that," said Coyote. "Wait and be ready. Just in case..."

That made Frog happy. He squatted
down by the pond and he waited while
the others set off along the trail through
the forest that led to the Fire Beings'
mountain-top.

On the way Coyote stopped from time
to time and told one of the animals to
wait beside the trail. First Squirrel, next
Chipmunk and then Deer were left
behind, and at last Bear and Coyote
walked on alone.

When they reached the tepee on the top
of the mountain, Coyote told Bear to wait
in the shadows until he heard Coyote call
"Aooo!" Then Bear must make a big
loud rumpus.

Coyote crept up to the tepee. He gave a
soft bark, and one of the Fire Beings
opened the flap and looked out.

Coyote sort of trembled and said in his quietest, most polite voice, "My legs are freezing cold. May I please put them inside your warm tepee?"

He was so exceedingly polite that the Fire Being said, "Ye-es, all right..."

Coyote stepped in his front legs and
then he stepped in his back legs. Then he
whisked in his tail! He looked longingly at
the great blazing fire in the centre of the
tepee but he said nothing. He just lay
down and closed his eyes as if he were
going to sleep. But the next moment he
gave a long Coyote call, "Aooo-ooo!"

From outside the tepee came the sound
of a big loud rumpus as Bear growled and
stamped about.

The Fire Beings all rushed out shouting, "Who's that?" And when they saw the Bear, they chased him.

Coyote was ready. He grabbed a piece of burning wood between his teeth, and away he ran, out of the tepee and down the mountain.

As soon as the Fire Beings saw Coyote with the firebrand, they chased him.

Coyote ran and ran. He was fast, but the Fire Beings were faster, and they came closer.

Then Coyote saw Deer. "Catch it and run!" he called and threw the firebrand.

Deer caught it and ran. But he ran so fast that the wind fanned the fire out behind him, and a flame jumped on to his long tail and burned most of it. So that's why Deer has a shortish tail, even today.

Deer was fast, but the Fire Beings were faster, and they came closer.

Then Deer saw Chipmunk, "Catch it and run!" he called, and threw the firebrand.

Chipmunk caught it and ran. But the Fire Beings came closer and closer, until one of them reached out an arm and clawed his back and left three long black stripes. And that's why Chipmunk has stripes on his back, even today.

Then Chipmunk saw Squirrel. "Catch it and run!" he called, and threw the firebrand.

Squirrel caught it and ran. But the firebrand had been burning fast and was now so short that its great heat made Squirrel's tail curl up over his back. And that's why Squirrel has a curled-up tail, even today.

Squirrel came to the pond. The Fire Beings were right at his back. What could he do?

Then he saw small, squatty Frog, waiting and ready. Just in case...

"Catch it and jump!" called Squirrel and threw the firebrand which was now quite tiny.

Frog caught the firebrand, but as he jumped one of the Fire Beings grabbed his tail and pulled it off. And that's why Frog has no tail, even today.

Now when Frog jumped, he landed in the pond, and to save the flames from the water, he gulped down the tiny firebrand.

He held his breath, and he swam over to
the other side of the pond.

Then Frog saw a tree. "Catch it and
hide!" he called and coughed up all that
was left of the firebrand, just a few bright
flames. And the tree caught the fire and
hid it.

The Fire Beings ran round the pond, and they looked for the fire. But it was hidden in the tree and they didn't know how to get it out again, so they returned to their home, high on the mountain-top.

But Coyote, who is wise, knew how to get fire out of the tree. He knew how to rub two dry sticks together to make a spark that could be fed with pine needles and pine cones and grow into a fire. It was Coyote who taught the people to do this, so that they need not be cold, ever again, in wintertime. And it was Coyote who went around and gave some fire to all the other trees, so that fire lies hidden in every tree, even today.

(A North American Indian story)